World-Building:
Crafting Immersive Story Worlds.
A Beginner's Guide

ISBN: 979-8-218-90293-3

Published by Catherine Medina
Tallahassee, Florida

This book is intended for educational and informational purposes only.

Printed in the United States of America.
First edition.

Table of Contents

Before You Begin

The Ordinary Things

Have you ever read a fictional book and forgot it wasn't real? Or wondered if the backstory was based on real history? Every story, no matter how imagined, has real-life elements. The possibility that it could be true is how readers are immersed into the story. Readers need something tangible, something that feels familiar, to make them believe. It is the inclusion of the most ordinary details in real life that convinces readers that world is real. If a reader can relate to the ordinary things, then why not the extraordinary things too?

The most ordinary things about our lives are often the things we never truly think about again. Family recipes we know like the back of our hand. Words we pronounce incorrectly every time we say them. That empty house on the corner of 2nd and 4th avenue that no one will buy or talk about. These types of ordinary details—ordinary because time has worn them down into just another mundane thing in our life—explain characters and their lifestyle. So, while becoming a great observer, don't forget to put yourself on the list of people to observe.

The Importance of Observation

Observation is an underrated skill that novice writers often ignore. There is a gold mine of details at your disposal, and guess where it is? Right in front of you. The most imaginative writers ground their stories with things they've seen and experienced. Think about J.R.R. Tolkien's description of the Shire in *The Lord of the Rings*: small but beautiful; densely populated with fertile, green, well-tilled land. Sound familiar? Sounds a little like the West Midlands of England, long before industrialization. Go figure, an Englishman describing the English countryside in his stories. And with so much precision that we can step right into those scenes.

The power of detail isn't just about tangible elements; sometimes it's history humming beneath a story. In *Song of Solomon*, a single offhand reference to racial violence prompts readers to remember the death of Emmett Till. This real-life event pulsates through the characters' choices—showing how historical details can give a story deeper motive without becoming the story itself. Echoes of real history don't have to be the plot to provide motive and texture. Readers can relate to the characters' reactions. Observation includes keeping tabs on the world. Current events, cultural shifts, and collective memory become great detail material because the history and headlines of a moment can also pull a reader in, even after the details start to become "murky" as the story continues.

Becoming an Observer

Becoming a good observer doesn't mean staring at people, following them, or violating anyone's privacy. It doesn't mean playing the role of an undercover PI hiding behind trash cans or standing outside someone's window on family game night—observation and decency must work together.

Being a good observer means noticing how the world ticks in short moments: how someone carries their coffee on a Monday morning, how a tired parent juggles groceries and a child on a Friday night, the way someone hangs their coat after a long day. What is the state of their clothing? What are their facial expressions? What does the coffee smell like? Keep a small notebook, or a journal, or use your phone and jot down the bare bones—what you see, hear, and smell. Short notes are best here because you're just collecting material, not writing scenes.

This habit of observation helps you build a warehouse of details that you can pick and pull anytime you need to. Some stuff will fit one story, some won't fit anyway, and that's normal. The point is to have more than what you need.

Below is a list of short, easy exercises: pick one for the week, repeat it daily, then practice blending—drop a single detail into a paragraph and show it; don't explain.

Training Your Eye Exercises

The Co ee Test: Watch three different people carry a hot drink. Note posture, speed, and how they hold the cup. What does their walk tell you about their mood or job? How might one small change (a spill, a sudden stop) reveal character?

Neighborhood Sounds: Step outside in the early morning or late at night. Sit quietly and listen. Set a timer. Write down five sounds and what they make you feel. Be specific. Which sound would a child remember first? Which sound could become a symbol in a scene?

The Grocery Store Game: Try to catch a loud conversation in line. Write two lines exactly as you hear them. Notice the rhythm, the words chosen, and what they could reveal about those people. What can you infer about the speakers' relationship? How would changing one word change the meaning?

Object Detail: Pick one small, everyday object in your home (a shoe, a mug, a key). Describe it in three sensory details. No backstory, just the object. What condition is it in? What's its purpose? What might this object say about its owner?

Summary

Observation takes practice. Building a warehouse of details takes time. After you've started collecting real-life details, stretch them, mix them, test-run them. Your details should do two things at once: set the scene and reveal character or conflict. Be selective.

Welcome

Stories of all genres shape our understanding of the world. Stories keep our memories intact and help us pass history to the next generation. They help us make sense of our lives and bring us together. Whether you're writing fiction, a memoir, or folklore, world-building is where creativity meets intention. It's not enough to come up with a good idea. Your idea needs a map or a guide, so that it doesn't wander off into aimless territory. Equally important, your story needs a world that readers can step into and meet your characters face-to-face, so to speak.

Story building is the process of developing core components that bring a story to life. That process includes character development, plotting, conflicts, and more. Story **world-building is the process of developing the settings behind the story.** Think of world-building as your blueprint, and you are the architect. Construction can't begin without a solid design. Every writer can benefit greatly from outlining the elements that give stories life and structure. After all, characters wandering around a poorly defined world can confuse readers and weaken your message. This workbook encourages flexibility while providing you with the tools to shape your vision.

How to Use This Workbook

This workbook is a toolbox, not a checklist. Not every exercise will make it into your final draft—and that's okay. In fact, being picky about what you use is encouraged. For your story, your character's whole world might be the house she grew up in, and she never left. If that's the case, you won't need the "Incorporating Multiple Dimensions or Realms" section, will you? Take only what you need for your blueprint. Nothing more.

During your world-building journey, it's important to remember that your readers can think for themselves. Adding too many details can do more harm than good. It's easy to want to include every single detail of the world we're building, but obsessive detailing can be distracting. Too many details can **be** just as harmful as not having enough. For example:

> See Spot, the small brown-and-white terrier with a frayed red collar and a limp from last winter's icy chase, run frantically across the uneven gravel driveway toward the squeaky iron gate at the end of the yard.

Quite a bit of details in there! And while it creates an in-depth visual of the scene and the character, the sense of urgency is lost. Now compare that example to this one:

> See Spot race frantically towards the squeaky iron gate at the end of the yard.

Urgency is back, and there are still some visual details left to help paint the scene. A good rule of thumb is to first start with the bare bones ("See Spot run"). If the scene feels incomplete, build it one detail at a time.

In this workbook, each section is designed to help you pick and choose the elements your story needs to thrive. There's no "right" way to use this workbook. There is no particular order you should follow. Move around, skip pages, and repeat exercises if that's what you need. This is *your* story and *your* process.

Let's start building.

The Foundations of World-Building

Congratulations on beginning this exciting adventure! The first step is usually the hardest one, so pat yourself on the back for getting started.

Before you can build a living, breathing world, you need to understand why it exists and what purpose it serves in your story. This section helps you lay the groundwork—not by mapping every mountain or naming every village, but by defining the meaning, tone, and boundaries of your world. Think of it as creating the foundation before the walls go up.

You'll begin by identifying your story's purpose and genre, the emotional tone that shapes its mood, and the scope of your world—how large or intimate this world feels to your reader. From there, you'll explore the role of conflict, the reader's perspective, and how to strike a balance between the familiar and the new. Each concept gives you tools to anchor your imagination and build upon the foundation.

By the end of this section, you'll create your own World-Building Statement—a short paragraph that defines what your world is really about. This becomes your compass for everything that follows. Whenever details start to drift or overwhelm, you can return to this statement to regain focus and direction.

In short, this section ensures that every creative choice—from tone to terrain—supports the heart of your story.

Establishing Purpose

Establishing the purpose of your story is important because it provides direction. It helps you keep a goal in mind even if you're unsure of how the story will end. For example, if you're writing a story about loss, your story's purpose might be to showcase the grief process, what it looks like (or feels like) to lose a parent or a lover. This could be a story that helps someone make sense of what they're going through during times of loss. Maybe that's its purpose. How does this relate to world-building? A story should unfold in spaces that amplify the character's journey through grief, such as a funeral home or the home of the lost one.

Dorothy Sayers emphasized the importance of a writer's intention. She encouraged writers to discover their intentions by asking: What truth does your story demand to be told? (*The Mind of the Marker*, 1941) Clarity like that can shape your story world by challenging you to make sure every detail aligns with the message you want to convey.

Deciding the purpose behind your story doesn't have to be a trivial thing. Sometimes the purpose unfolds after you begin to write. It happens. But once you get there, that clarity will keep you focused as the story unfolds. Then, the details of your story will support the setting, rather than distract from it. When every detail is rooted in your story's purpose, they enhance the narrative.

What do you think will influence this story?

Example: A personal experience, ancient myths, recent historical event, etc.

What theme(s) will this story explore and why?

Example: [Mystery writer] This story will explore the theme of truth—how chasing it can expose not just secrets, but the parts of ourselves we'd rather keep hidden.

Why is this story important to you?
What will make it important to readers?

Example: [Comic book writers] *This story matters to me because it lets me turn power, fear, and courage into living symbols—so readers can see their own struggles in the hero behind the mask.*

How might your world challenge or comfort your readers?

Example: [Fantasy writers] *My world might challenge readers by showing them that even magic has consequences—and that courage often means choosing mercy over power.*

Establishing Tone & Genre

Genre defines the stylistic direction of a story, while tone shapes its emotional atmosphere. Genre provides the rules and expectations—fantasy, sci-fi, historical, mystery—so you know what kinds of events, technologies, or impossibilities the world is likely to contain. Those choices guide your plot, the types of conflicts you'll stage, and the logic you'll need to maintain throughout the story.

Genre also affects the concrete details you choose. A historical novel needs specific foods, clothing, and day-to-day routines that are true to fact; a detective story needs clues, urban layout, and procedural habits; a fantasy piece may require invented rituals or economies. These choices set the framework for the genre, so readers understand what isn't allowed and what to look forward to.

Tone tells the reader how to feel about the world you've shown them. Is your story eerie, playful, ironic, hopeful, or bleak? Tone comes from word choice, sentence rhythm, and the small sensory details you've gathered in your warehouse. John Updike's writing in *Rabbit, Run* shows how a single domestic image can set tone and reveal inner life: "Her apartment smells of dust and kitchen grease and herself, a little sharp like sweat, a little soft like powder." (Updike, 64) That line does more than describe a room; it establishes intimacy and a discomfort that shapes how we see both the character and her living space.

Deciding on genre and tone early helps everything else fall into place. A lighthearted sci-fi is usually bright in its visuals and quick in its cadence; gritty post-apocalyptic tales favor muted colors, blunt verbs, and hard, practical details. Also, let's not overlook how important consistency is after the choices are made. The consistency of a specific genre's rules also helps make your world believable.

What genre have you decided your story will be?

Example: [Historical fiction writer]: My story will be historical fiction, because I want to reimagine forgotten voices and show how the past still shapes the present.

What tone do you want your world to possess?

Example: Quietly melancholic—the world feels soft at first, but under that softness is a steady sadness (short sentences, muted colors, lots of rainy scenes).

Visualizing the Look & Scope

The scale of your world shapes what your characters can explore. A small, focused world—like a single town—enables deep emotional intimacy and rich community dynamics. A larger world, such as a sprawling multiverse, allows for grand adventures and complex cultural landscapes.

Without clarity on size, it's easy to overbuild or leave gaps while writing the first drafts of your story. Determining whether your story takes place in one location or spans multiple galaxies creates a roadmap for what for you'll need to focus on, such as pacing, various details, and any research you might need to do beforehand. The scope you choose should align with the stakes—larger stakes require a broader world, while smaller, personal stakes allow for a more intimate setting.

Equally important is visualizing how your world will look. Literary critic Percy Lubbock praised writers for giving their novels a *defined aesthetic*, saying, "…   The art of fiction does not begin until the novelist thinks of his story as a matter to be shown, to be so exhibited that it will tell itself" (*The Craft of Fiction,* 1921). A clear visual style—colors, textures, shapes, and architecture—ground your world. Visual elements also influence the emotional tone of your story. Dark, muted imagery suggests mystery or bleakness, while vibrant visuals convey wonder or joy. A sleek city of steel and glass indicates a high-tech society, while crumbling ruins hint at a fallen civilization.

How large is your world?

Which regions or locations are crucial to your story?

What visual elements best describe your world?

 Salt-streaked roofs, narrow cobbled alleys, markets hung with dried fish and faded flags, and low, fog-filled mornings.

The Role of Conflict

Your story world can give your conflict more momentum. Conflict shapes your plot, but your story controls the terrain your characters navigate. When conflict is embedded in the world itself, those terrains move beyond background noise. A well-crafted world doesn't just hold the story; it pushes back against it. It challenges your characters, limits their choices, and makes them adapt. A desert world might test endurance; a rigid society might punish small acts of defiance. These pressures—these do not have to become the story—create tension and reveal character through action even as the real story goes on. When the world resists, too, the story moves into a space of realism.

Political tensions, environmental disasters, and supernatural threats create dynamics that shape your setting. A divided empire may create zones of oppression and rebellion, and neighborhoods might become battlegrounds. A natural disaster can reshape lands and displace the people who once called it home. These forces impact architecture, social structures, and human (or alien) relations. Conflict can transform peaceful villages into war camps or sacred lands into battlegrounds.

Conflict isn't just what your characters face—it's what your world expresses. By building tension into the very fabric of your setting, you give your story a driving force. Your world becomes an active player.

Think about your story's purpose and the troubles your character will face on the journey.

How will that conflict shape the world they live in?

What is the central conflict?

Where is this conflict most visible in the physical world?

Does this conflict change people's daily lives? How?

What physical barriers exist because of this conflict?

If your conflict is solved, how would the physical structure of your world change? What scars would remain?

Does your story have more than one conflict?

Use this page to include an additional conflict.

What is the secondary conflict?

Is there a connection between your secondary conflict and the central conflict?

How does it affect your character's behavior, routines, and relationships?

What physical barriers exist because of this conflict?

Understanding the Reader's Journey

Planning the reader's journey means considering how your world unfolds through the story's pacing, perspective, and details. Readers latch onto touchpoints they can quickly imagine because they're familiar—marketplaces, red brick walls, landmarks. Even referencing actual events, like World War II, can help a reader quickly imagine a war zone and move on with the story.

Even if your world is vast, your reader has to enter it one step at a time, and the first step is crucial. The first should do both things: pull them in and keep them. Each scene should be anchored in familiar details, accompanied by something unexpected. Together, these elements make the strange feel possible and meaningful.

A reader's experience is just as important as your character's. Start your reader with one clear, relatable detail that opens the world rather than trying to show everything at once. Let new facts arrive like clues—one small piece at a time—so curiosity grows instead of confusion. Vary the pace: slow down to let a strange custom sink in, speed up when action should push the plot forward. Use point of view to control what readers know and when they know it; a close perspective can make tiny, intimate details feel huge. Be intentional about what you hide and what you reveal—mystery is earned, not random. Connect surprises to things the reader already understands so novelty feels possible, not arbitrary. Do this well, and your world won't just be described on the page; it will feel like a place the reader walks through, learning as they go.

Where does the reader first enter your world? What will they see, hear, and smell first?

How will the world be revealed to the reader?

Balancing Familiarity & Novelty

A well-built world strikes a balance between the comfort of familiar things and the thrill of the unknown. Readers are naturally drawn to settings that echo real-life experiences and recognizable tropes—castles, cities, or social systems. These touchpoints make it easier for readers to understand your world and become immersed in it.

However, if everything feels too familiar, your story might lose its uniqueness. Novelty can set your work apart. Strange customs, unique magic rules, odd character traits, hybrid cultures, or unexplained technology make readers curious. In contrast, too much innovation without a clear anchor can feel confusing. The most successful stories strike a balance, offering just enough newness to surprise while still giving readers something to relate to.

In *One Hundred Years of Solitude*, Gabriel García Márquez built Macondo, a town whose physical sensations are deeply familiar: heat, tropical vegetation, family homes, and generational conflicts. He then layers in remarkable, surprising elements: rains that last for years, ghostly figures who return from death, Remedios the Beauty who rises to the sky in broad daylight, and so on. These extraordinary events are woven into the narrative with the same steady tone as ordinary life. Readers aren't jolted by them. They're gradually drawn into accepting the peculiar as part of the lived reality of Macondo. That mix—a familiar foundation plus ever-deepening marvels—makes the strange both acceptable and emotionally resonant.

What familiar elements will ground your world?

 Daily routines like morning coffee, gossip at the bakery, and a child's game—these make the setting human before introducing its strange laws.

What makes your world feel fresh and unique?

 Fish that sing in the moonlight…

Defining Your World:
A World-building Statement

A world-building statement serves as the foundation of your fictional world. It defines the core principles, rules, and tone that shape your setting, clarifying what your world is—and what it isn't. This short, focused declaration keeps your vision on track, even when new ideas or unexpected story developments arise.

It's also a practical tool for crafting. By referencing your statement, you can evaluate whether cultures, conflicts, technologies, or magic systems fit within the structure you've set. Whether working alone or collaborating, it communicates the essence of your world to editors, beta readers, or creative partners, ensuring everyone stays aligned.

Consistency flows naturally from a strong world-building statement. Clear rules and boundaries make it easier to maintain internal logic, keeping readers engaged and immersed. Tools like world bibles, timelines, and maps can help track details, but your statement is the anchor that holds everything together.

A world-building statement gives a solid structure to build your world on top of, helping you keep track of what belongs and what doesn't. It keeps your ideas focused and your rules and laws consistent. Even as your story grows and changes, this statement acts as a steady guide, making it easier to craft a coherent, immersive world that feels real and engaging.

What core principles define your world?

What core principles define your world?

What are the rules that govern your world?

How would you describe your world in one or two sentences?

Checkpoint

Let's pause. Gather your thoughts and answers from the previous section and use this checkpoint to put it all together.

- Use the following charts to collect your ideas.

- Summarize your overall purpose.

- Describe your "why" for building this world.

- List key themes you want to explore.

- Decide on the tone and genre for your story.

- Summarize your visual style and the scope of the world

As a reminder, it's important not to overdo it. Not every question asked will apply to the goal you want to reach. Don't be afraid to leave some boxes empty.

Your story's purpose influences the entire story. Readers can tell when a story is aimless. You must decide what the message is and how you want to convey it. Use the boxes below to begin outlining the details that define your story.

The conflict in your story will shape the environment your characters inhabit. Decide what they will struggle to resolve and how that conflict will influence their physical world.

(Note: You do not need three con icts in one story.)

Conflict #1	Conflict #2	Conflict #3

Influence(s)	Influence(s)	Influence(s)

Draft the first scene that your readers will enter. Include only the physical detail. What details will your readers see, smell, or hear first?

Refer to the warehouse of real-life details you've hopefully been building. On this page, fill in each box, picking details that will fuel your story, not distract from it.

Consider: smell, sounds, textures, gestures, habits, behaviors, etc.

Familiar / Relatable	Novelty / New

Consistency is the backbone of a convincing immersive world. The rules must apply to everyone. On this page, decide which core principles and regulations will govern your world. What will be the cultural expectations, the legal laws, and the laws of physics?

Core Principles:
Beliefs and values that guide action.

World Rules:
specific directives that dictate action.

Before you continue, writing is a creative and mental workout. Just like any muscle in the body, your mind needs rest to recharge, regain perspective, and stay productive. Taking intentional breaks from your writing process isn't about slacking off—it's a tool that can make your storytelling stronger.

Stepping away from your project gives your subconscious time to work through creative blocks. While you're taking a break, your brain is still sorting out story problems and sparking new ideas.

Breaks also help prevent burnout. Writing for too long without rest can lead to frustration, doubt, or tunnel vision. By creating space between drafting sessions, you return to your work with a sharper focus and a rested mind. It also gives you a chance to read, live life, or observe the world around you—don't forget your warehouse.

So, remember: **rest is productive**. It's a key part of the process, not a delay.

Geography, Climate & Scenery

Every story takes place somewhere—and that "somewhere" shapes everything that happens within it. This section helps you design the physical backbone of your world: its landforms, environments, and the systems that sustain life there. Geography influences more than scenery; it determines how people live, what they value, and how they adapt.

You'll explore how to define the shape of the land, develop believable ecosystems and resources, and understand the contrast between urban and rural environments. These decisions give your world texture and rhythm, revealing how culture, economy, and even storytelling traditions evolve from the ground up.

Rather than rushing to fill in every detail, this section encourages you to decide only what the story truly needs. A single mountain range might isolate a civilization for centuries, while a river could become a symbol of migration or change. Each choice adds both logic and emotion to your setting.

By the end, you'll have a landscape that feels purposeful and alive—a place your readers can see, smell, and believe in. The aim isn't to build a map for its own sake, but to build a world that moves your characters and your readers alike.

Shape of the Land

The geography of your world shapes far more than scenery—it defines how people live, trade, travel, and survive. Mountains may isolate communities and preserve old traditions, while coasts invite exchange, migration, and conflict. Harsh deserts, fertile valleys, and frozen tundras all create their own kinds of people, stories, and challenges. When your geography makes sense, your world feels real. Every path, river, and border gives readers a sense that this place has existed long before the story began.

Tolkien often wrote about how closely his stories and settings were linked. In *The Fellowship of the Ring*, the Fellowship's failed attempt to cross the Misty Mountains—and their fateful decision to go through the Mines of Moria when the snow made the pass impossible—shows how the land itself can shape the story's direction. Geography, in this way, isn't just your character's physical surroundings; it's an invisible hand guiding the plot and the choices your characters make.

Climate and weather deepen this realism. The same land can feel completely different depending on its temperature, storms, and seasons. In *A Farewell to Arms*, rain becomes a symbol of despair and loss, ending with the haunting image of the protagonist walking away "in the rain" after tragedy strikes (Hemingway 332). When used intentionally, weather can echo emotion, foreshadow conflict, or heighten the reader's sense of unease. It turns the landscape into an emotional mirror.

Natural elements—sunlight, wind, fog, storms—add tone to every scene. A blinding blizzard can trap a character both physically and psychologically. A humid summer afternoon can make tempers flare. When the natural world reacts in rhythm with your characters' struggles, it grounds the story in something readers can feel. A well-shaped land and believable climate make your world breathe. They show that environment and emotion are not separate things—they're reflections of each other.

What natural landscapes dominate your world?

Example: *Mangrove swamps near the shore, chalk cliffs that crumble in storms, and a central marsh that people avoid because of old legends.*

How does geography affect how people live, move, and connect with others?

Example: *Villages cling to the coast and trade by boat; inland communities are isolated in the hills and trade salt and wool via long caravans.*

How do seasons or weather shape your story's events or mood?

Example: A harsh winter forces rival groups to share a mountain pass, creating tension and unexpected alliances.

How can you use the natural world to reflect your protagonist's inner state?

Example: A clear sunrise after a storm mirrors the moment your character finds forgiveness or clarity.

Natural Resources & Imaginary Ecosystems

Once you've set the map and the weather, fill the map with life. The Living Land is about what grows, what can be mined, what drinks the rivers, and what creatures walk the fields—because those things decide how people survive, trade, fight, and worship. Water, soil, metals, and food shape towns and trade routes; a place with abundant timber builds differently from a place that must import wood. Scarcity makes rules and hard choices; abundance creates opportunity and, sometimes, entitlement.

Ecosystems do more than supply goods. Plants and animals become tools, medicine, and myth. A healing herb can be sacred; a dangerous predator can be woven into law and ritual. When people depend on a single resource, that dependence becomes a lens for everything else: class, law, marriage alliances, and who gets to speak at council. The way a society organizes itself—who controls the wells, who owns the mines, who tends the fields—tells you what that culture prizes and fears.

A living, believable ecology also creates practical problems and story engines: disease that spreads through trade routes, a crop failure that forces migration, a newly discovered ore that redraws borders. These are not abstract plot devices; they are consequences that grow from the land you designed. Let the biology and resources push your plot: if a river is dammed, show the downstream town's anger; if a fungus blights a staple crop, show how markets, priests, and rebels respond. When the world's life affects daily choices, the story feels earned.

Finally, treat ecosystems as systems, not props. Ask how species interact, what eats what, and how people fit into that web. The tighter you tie culture and economy to ecology, the more inevitable and lived-in your world will feel.

Which natural resources are abundant or scarce in your world?

Example: Fresh groundwater is rare inland, so caravans and cisterns control travel and trade.

What species, plants, or ecological features are unique to your world, and how do people use or revere them?

Example: A slow-growing reed is the only material that holds certain dyes; it is harvested once a decade and reserved for ceremonial robes.

How do resources shape power and daily life?

 Control of a salt flat funds the coastal governor's court and lets them hire private guards, widening the gap between city and countryside.

What environmental change could force large-scale social or political shifts?

 Receding fish stocks collapse a fishing town's economy and push young people to migrate to the city, shifting demographics and voting blocs.

Urban vs. Rural Settings

Exploring both urban and rural settings adds contrast to your world-building. These spaces reflect different values, lifestyles, and power dynamics within your story. Cities concentrate people, institutions, money, and rapid change: problems show up fast, laws ripple widely, and systems (courts, markets, bureaucracy) shape everyday life. Rural areas hold different strengths: local knowledge, food production, slow-but-strong social ties, and long memories that cities often forget. Those differences create obvious story mechanics (migration, resource grabs, policy clashes) and quieter, deeper effects (belief systems, inherited grudges, ritual practices).

When choosing one or the other, also think about zones of transition. The road between port and farmland, the train that brings migrants, the border town where languages mix are especially fertile. These liminal places let worlds touch: deals are struck, smuggling routes open, marriages happen, and small, decisive confrontations arise that feel natural to the place. Anchor each location with a few specific, recurring details (a sound, a smell, a time of day, an everyday object) so the contrast is felt as texture, not explained as exposition.

When urban and rural worlds collide, the result should push plot and test characters. A city policy that seems logical from the capital's viewpoint might ruin a village economy; a factory's waste can poison a river that feeds several towns; migration can empty fields and flood tenements. These are the kinds of conflicts that feel earned because they grow out of place. Use those contrasts to create believable pressure on your characters and to reveal the values and faults of the society you're building.

Which area would better suit your story? Why?

In what ways can you use these settings to drive your story?

Checkpoint

Let's pause. Gather your thoughts and answers from the previous section and use this checkpoint to put it all together. You've mapped mountains, rivers, deserts, and cities. You've felt how climate shapes daily life and how resources and ecosystems create opportunities and challenges. You've explored the contrast between bustling towns and quiet countryside, and how those spaces refl ect culture, values, and rhythm.

- Summarize the geographical features. What regions and landscapes have you outlined?

- List the key locations. How are these locations connected to the story?

- Describe the landscapes. Include details of the fl ora, fauna, and atmospheric conditions that set the mood.

- Summarize how climate, weather, and seasonal variations shape your world.

Organization is always key! Mapping key locations allows you to track how characters move through the world and establish the relationships between them. Use these blank pages to decide which key location or locations are and how they connect to the story. List them, draw them; do whatever helps you get a clear picture.

History, Culture & Society

Every world has a past—and that past shapes everything your characters believe, build, and become. In this section, you'll explore how the passage of time and the weight of tradition give depth to your world. History isn't just background; it's a living influence that explains how things came to be and what might change next.

You'll begin by building your world's history, tracing the key events that shaped nations, communities, and ideas. From there, you'll explore myths, legends, and folklore, uncovering how people explain the unexplainable. These stories often reveal a culture's fears, hopes, and moral compass.

Next, you'll examine social structures and hierarchies, understanding how power, class, and identity determine who thrives—and who struggles—in your world. Finally, you'll look at the economy, where trade, scarcity, and innovation shape daily life.

Together, these elements form the heartbeat of your world. They turn settings into societies and populations into people. By the end of this section, you'll know not just what your world looks like—but how it remembers, organizes, and sustains itself.

Building Your World's History

History gives your world context and life. It explains why societies behave the way they do, why conflicts persist, and how cultures evolve. Even small details from the past—wars, migrations, revolutions, or discoveries—leave traces that affect language, customs, beliefs, and daily routines. When you understand the history of your world, your setting feels lived-in and believable.

Creating a timeline of key events helps you organize this history. Map out milestones like the founding of a kingdom, major battles, technological breakthroughs, or social revolutions. Think about how these events shape the present: a long-ago war could still influence trade, diplomacy, or alliances, and a golden age of innovation might explain why certain cities thrive. Gaps or mysteries in history are also useful—they can spark curiosity, give characters secrets to uncover, and provide opportunities for tension or plot twists.

History isn't just dates and events—it's also personal. Characters are shaped by what came before them, whether through family legacies, cultural traditions, or lingering societal tensions. Have you ever read *The Kite Runner* by Khaled Hosseini? The framework of Afghanistan's civil war and the rise of the Taliban profoundly shape the characters' identities and decisions, influencing the plot's trajectory. A well-integrated past makes characters' actions and decisions feel natural and rooted in your world.

What key historical events shape your world?

Example: A king starved the poor, and a great rebellion overthrew his rule, leading to…

How did those shape current social norms and language/communication/linguistics?

Myths, Legends & Folklore

Myths, legends, and belief systems are how a people explain the world to themselves and how they choose to live in it. Small stories become sacred folklore. Origin myths tell why a river is holy or why a founding legend justifies a throne. Cautionary tales create taboos. Over time, those stories harden into rituals, laws, and superstitions: festivals, mourning rites, vows, and rules about who may speak in council. Belief systems give meaning to suffering and glue communities together (or split them apart).

Think of folklore and myths as the world's emotional map and belief systems as its operating system. One supplies color and memory; the other runs everyday life. Together, they shape art, authority, justice, and even trade—because what a culture reveres or fears will influence what it protects or exploits. When you weave myths and practices into your setting, you create layers of motive for characters: why someone risks everything for a relic, or why a village refuses to leave a floodplain. Those layers make scenes resonate beyond the plot; they let readers feel that your world has depth, history, and reasons for being.

What founding myth or legend do people tell about your world?

How do beliefs shape power or law in your world?

What small, everyday habit reveals a deeper cultural belief?

Social Structures & Hierarchies

The social structure of your world shapes power, relationships, and daily life. Whether built on strict hierarchies or loose alliances, it determines who makes decisions and who answers to whom. Class, status, and social roles create friction, and they affect access to resources, information, and opportunity. A society split by wealth may breed quiet resentments that erupt into rebellion; a merit-based culture can produce ruthless competition and subtle corruption. Social rules also steer how people show respect; those rituals tell you what a character will or won't tolerate.

That said, you don't need to publish an essay on your world's social theory. Unless your story specifically examines social systems and hierarchies, much of this detail is primarily for you, the author: a set of backstage rules that keep characters acting consistently throughout the story. Think of it as a shorthand—enough structure to explain why someone behaves honorably, why another lies, or why a crowd tolerates an injustice. Keep a few clear, memorable anchors (a law, a taboo, a title) and you'll be able to show class and status through action, not exposition.

How does your world's social structure influence your characters' opportunities or limitations?

Example: Only nobles can attend the academy where magic is taught, forcing commoners to seek outlawed teachers in secret.

How do these hierarchies affect interactions between people?

Example: People from different social classes might be forbidden from speaking to each other or have their interactions strictly governed.

The Economy of Your World

The economy shapes how people live and what they value. From simple barter systems to sprawling magical markets, trade defines the flow of goods and opportunity. It influences class mobility, regional relationships, and the rise or fall of entire civilizations. Unequal wealth can breed tension, while prosperity can bring complacency.

Economic systems can reveal a culture's mindset. What do people consider valuable—gold, grain, knowledge, magic, or honor? These priorities determine who thrives and who struggles. The way your world produces, trades, and consumes resources affects everything from daily survival to politics and war.

This is another element that doesn't need the spotlight. Sometimes, it's more of an invisible framework—something that helps maintain realism in the background. Knowing the basic rules of exchange, who profits, and who gets left behind enables you to write characters who are just as human as we are, even if readers never hear a word about taxes, trade routes, or currency.

What is the main economic system in your world? What's most valuable?

What is considered most valuable in your world, and why?

Checkpoint

Let's pause. Gather your thoughts and answers from the previous section and use this checkpoint to put it all together. Use the following steps to collect your ideas:

- Summarize the historical events and backstories that shape your world. What major milestones have influenced its current state?

- Outline your world's timeline. List key events and how they connect to the narrative's foundation.

- Describe how the myths and legends influence culture and daily life.

- Summarize the social structures, hierarchies, and economic systems in your world. What conflicts or alliances arise from these?

- Write down the language, beliefs, and cultural traditions. How do these elements support your narrative?

Use this chart to identify key historical events that occurred BEFORE your story takes place. These events should explain the cultural and social status of your story. Each event should lead up to the beginning of your story.

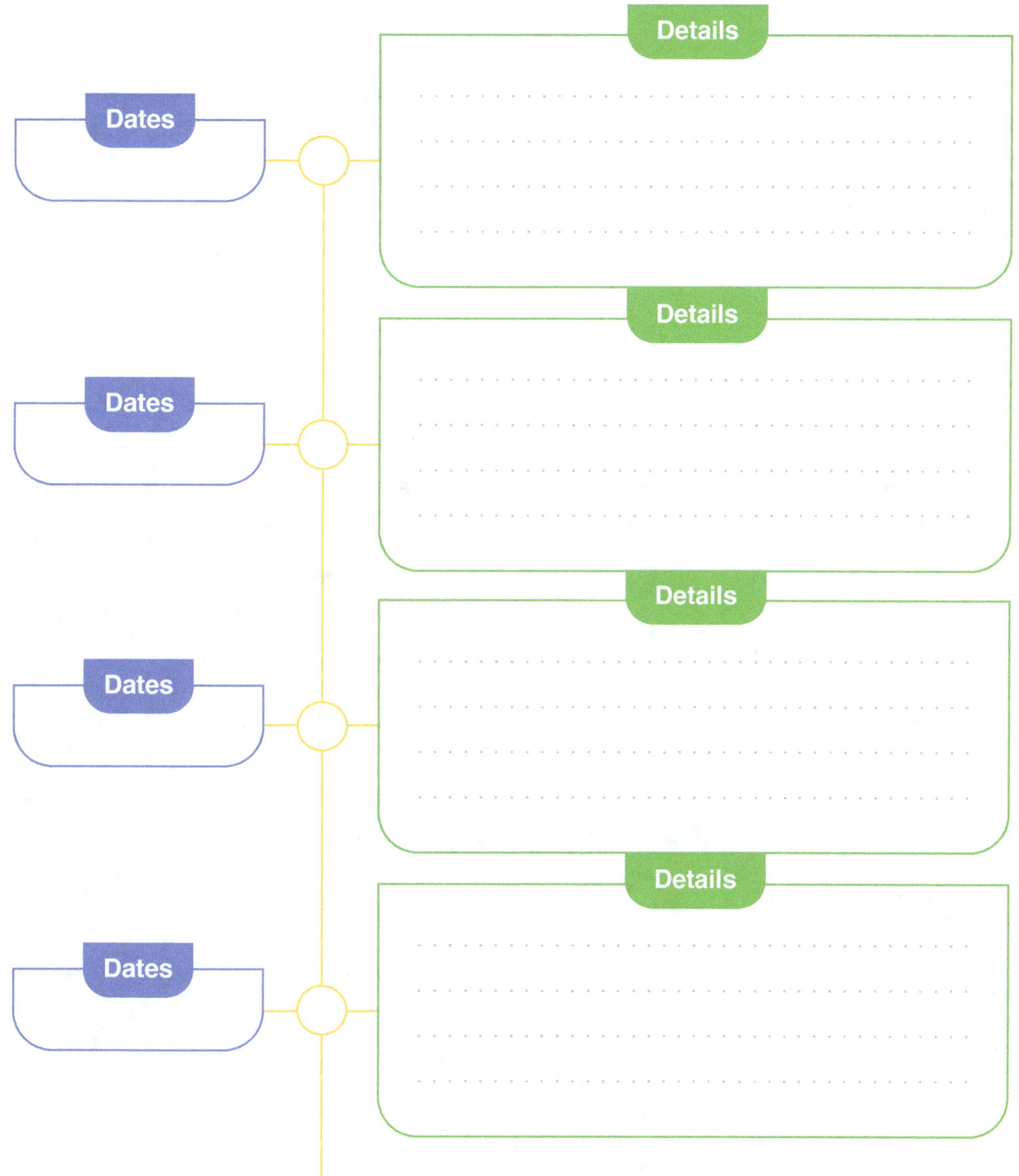

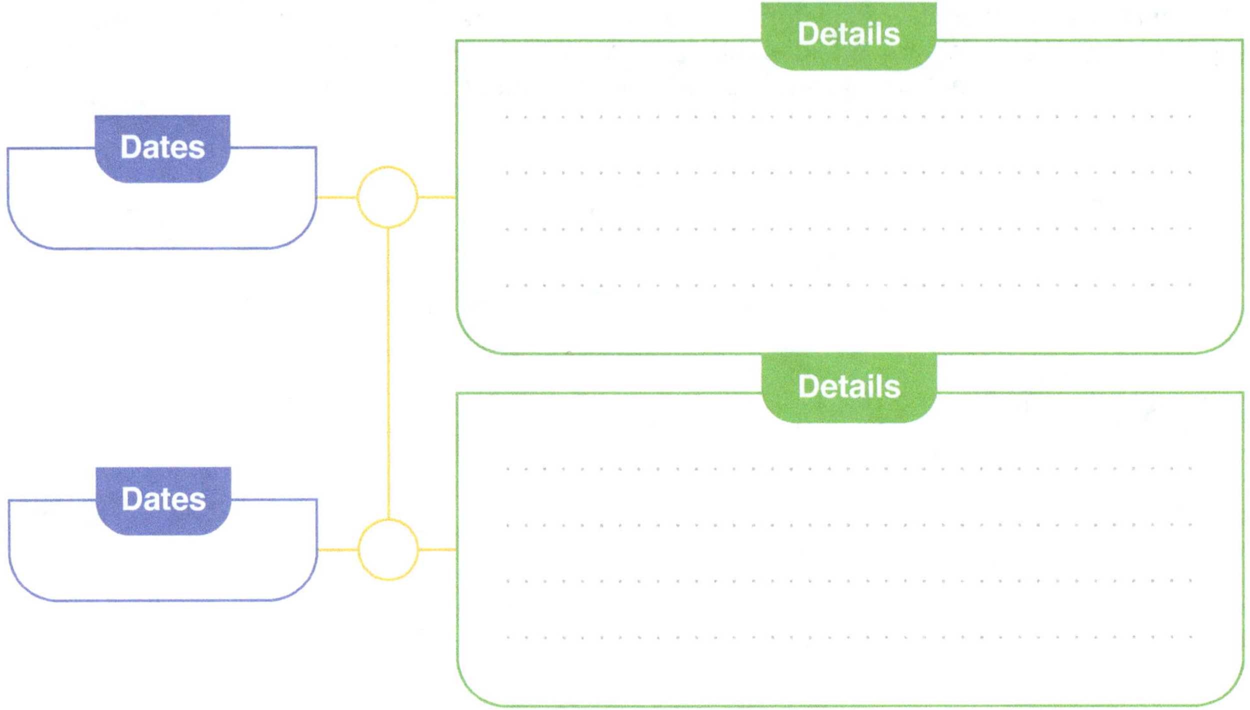

As you continue down this chart, begin to identify events that occur DURING your story.

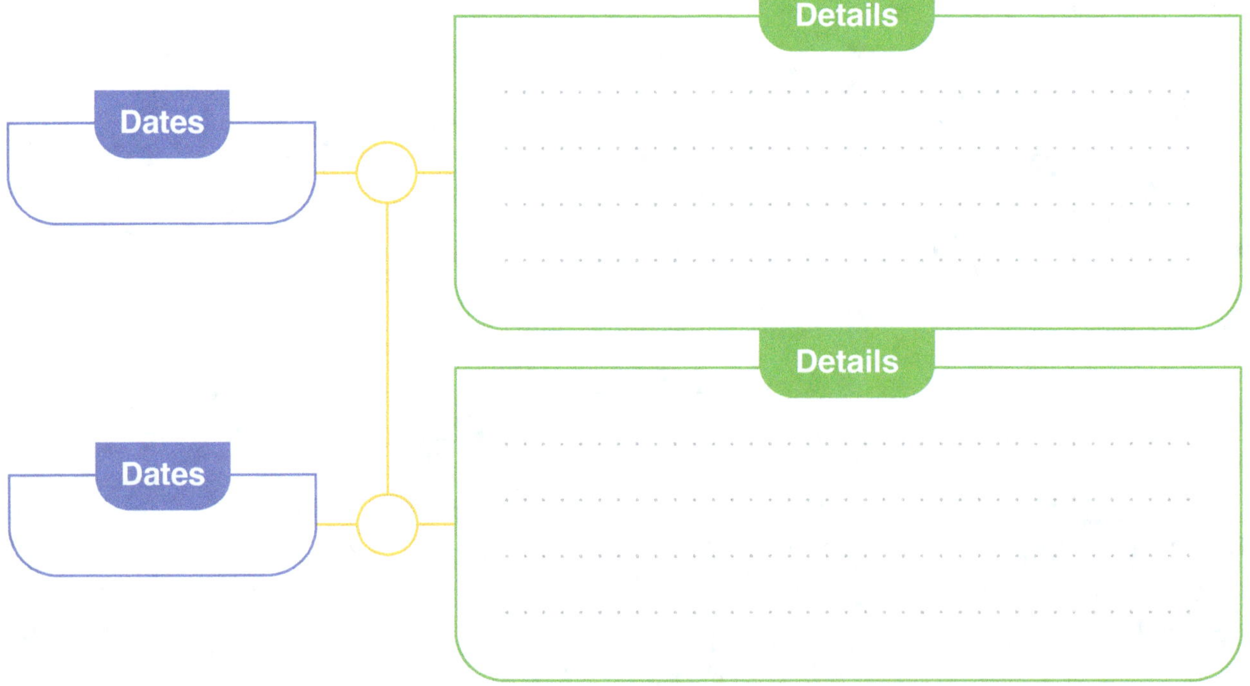

Dates
Dates
Dates
Dates
Details
Details
Details
Details

Before you continue:

By now, you've been deep in your world-building process—thinking hard, planning carefully, and shaping ideas into structure. Before moving forward, ask yourself: Is it break time? If so, take a moment to step away. Just like a muscle, your mind needs rest to recharge. This isn't about losing momentum; it's about gaining perspective.

A short break can refresh your focus, clear creative clutter, and make room for unexpected insights. Sometimes the best ideas surface when you're not staring at the page. Whether it's a walk, a nap, or a day spent doing something entirely different, time away often brings you back stronger.

Think of this as part of your rhythm: create, pause, return. Your story —and your mind—will thank you for it.

Section IV:
Unique Elements & Special Features

Every story world has something that makes it stand out—something readers will remember outside of the plot. Unique elements—whether magical forces, advanced technologies, rare plant life, or extraordinary character traits—bring a story to life. They don't *need* to be grand or flashy (but it's okay if they are); their impact comes from how they shape your world and affect your characters. A society built around a flower that blooms once a decade can feel just as rich as one defined by ancient spells or futuristic inventions. Even subtle details—a peculiar tradition, or an unusual weather pattern—can make your world feel alive and meaningful.

The key is thoughtful integration. Consider how each element influences daily life, social structures, or personal behavior. Do they affect laws, traditions, or relationships? Could they create opportunities for conflict or cooperation? When unique features are seamlessly woven into the fabric of your world, they deepen immersion and invite readers to explore the story on multiple levels.

In this chapter, we'll explore how to make your world feel real, consistent, and compelling. We'll look at rules and limitations, the behavior of time and space, multiple realms, mythical creatures, and hidden symbolism. By understanding how these pieces interact, you'll be able to craft a world that's not only vivid and memorable but also serves your story's themes and characters naturally.

Defining Rules & Limitations

Every story world has its own rules, whether it's magic, technology, or just the natural order of life. Without rules, powerful elements can feel like shortcuts, and story conflicts can disappear. By establishing limitations, you give your characters challenges to overcome and create consequences for their actions.

Blending science and fantasy in your world can make it feel rich and layered, but it requires consistency. All the rules and limits of your world must follow some logical pattern, so that readers can understand what's possible and what's not. Beforehand, decide how far these elements can go, how they interact, and what happens when rules are broken. When your rules are clear, the extraordinary feels earned rather than arbitrary, and conflicts naturally arise.

Think about how your rules shape daily life and character choices. Does magic require rare ingredients, skill, or sacrifice? Does technology have limits that affect trade, travel, or warfare? Are there scientific principles in your world that interact with magical systems in unexpected ways? Considering these details now ensures your story stays consistent, while giving you creative freedom to explore the extraordinary.

What are the rules or limitations of the unique elements in your world?

Example: Spells can only be cast at night, or only once per month, forcing characters to plan carefully.

How do these rules affect daily life or shape your characters' decisions?

Example: A magical energy source powers cities, but its scarcity causes tension between regions.

What consequences arise when rules are broken?

Example: Misusing a powerful artifact triggers natural disasters or social upheaval.

The Behavior of Time & Space

Time and space actively shape how your story functions. You decide what's normal or what behaves strangely due to magic or technology (or even culture). Time might be linear or looped, affecting character choices and consequences. Space can shift, distances can deceive, or locations can move, creating mystery and tension.

These elements can also add symbolism and emotional weight. A looping day might reflect a character's inner struggle. A shifting landscape can mirror freedom or isolation. Ted Chiang's *The Story of Your Life* treats time itself as fluid, influencing character perception and decision-making. (As Dr. Banks learns an alien language, she begins to perceive time differently: instead of seeing it linearly, past → present → future, she experiences time simultaneously.) Chiang's approach shows how time functions in a story can be central to plot, theme, and emotional impact.

How does time function in your world? How does it influence your character's decisions?

Are there unusual spatial rules or distortions?

Incorporating Multiple Dimensions or Realms

While multiple dimensions or realms can be an exciting narrative tool, they are not essential—or even appropriate—for every story. **The needs of the plot and its themes and tone should drive the decision to include multiple dimensions or realms**. Ask yourself: *Does this feature serve the heart of the story, or does it distract from it?* In genres like speculative fiction, fantasy, or surrealism, alternate realms often feel like a natural fit. For historical fiction, thrillers, or literary genres, adding this element might feel awkward and distracting to the reader.

The benefits of including multiple realms are vast. They allow writers to build layered, symbolic spaces that reflect emotional or philosophical tension. These alternate worlds can function as metaphors—representing internal conflict, societal divisions, or moral dilemmas. The contrast between realms can also highlight what is broken or missing in the "real" world and create opportunities for rich visual world-building, unexpected plot twists, and suspense.

However, successfully executing it (in any genre) requires careful thought and structure. Each realm must be distinct, with its own internal logic, rules, and consequences. Transitions between realms should feel purposeful, not arbitrary.

Done well, multiple dimensions can transform a story into a tapestry of ideas and experiences. Done poorly, they can dilute the impact and confuse the reader. The key is knowing *why* you're using them—and taking the time to develop every additional realm individually.

Does each realm have clear rules and logic?

Example: A shadow realm where time flows differently, affecting travel and communication.

How do transitions between realms impact the plot?

Example: Characters must pass through a dangerous portal, creating tension and higher stakes.

What opportunities for conflict or discovery arise from multiple realms?

Example: Rival factions occupy different realms, sparking clashes that affect the main world.

Mythical Creatures & Beings

Mythical creatures and beings are a hallmark of fantastical worlds, serving as symbols, challenges, or even allies for your characters. These beings can embody the forces of nature and/or represent societal ideals and challenges. Dragons, spirits, or shapeshifters are not just interesting additions to your world—they often reflect deep themes within your narrative. For instance, a dragon may symbolize greed or destruction, while a spirit might represent the connection between the living and the dead. These creatures can drive conflict, catalyze major plot points, or serve as metaphors for internal struggles within the characters. The unique roles that these beings play within your world can also help define societal norms and shape characters' destinies. Developing mythical creatures with intricate backstories and motivations adds layers of meaning to your world and narrative, making your setting feel both magical and alive.

What unique creatures populate your world?

Example: Dragons, spirits, or shapeshifters that have their own agendas

How do these beings reflect or challenge societal norms?

Example: A creature that is feared and revered in equal measure, representing both destruction and protection

In what ways can their existence contribute to the plot or symbolize themes?

Example: Their presence might catalyze conflicts or serve as metaphors for inner struggles.

Symbolism & Hidden Meanings

Symbols and hidden meanings enrich your world by adding depth to the narrative. They can serve as tools for foreshadowing, reflecting themes, or providing clues to characters and readers alike. Whether it's a recurring motif like a specific color, animal, or artifact, these symbols carry weight and influence how the story unfolds. For example, a recurring symbol might represent hope, a personal journey, or the passage of time. Symbols can also carry hidden meanings, known only to a select few, which can add mystery and intrigue to the narrative. By embedding symbolism into your world, you create layers of meaning that invite readers to explore beyond the surface. These hidden elements may reveal themselves gradually, enriching the reader's experience and offering opportunities for interpretation. Such symbols also create cohesion within your world, tying together seemingly unrelated elements and reinforcing the themes that define your story.

Use the following chart to infuse your world with symbols that resonate with broader themes. Consider hidden meanings behind recurring imagery.

Object
Description
Hidden Meaning
Object
Description
Hidden Meaning
Object
Description
Hidden Meaning

Merging Science with Fantasy

Blending science with fantasy creates a rich, multifaceted world that balances logic with imagination. This approach allows you to build a reality that feels grounded in some ways while still leaving room for wonder and possibility. By incorporating scientific principles into fantastical elements, you can create a world that feels both plausible and enchanting. For instance, you might alter the laws of physics in certain regions affected by magic, or you could integrate futuristic technology with ancient mysticism. This fusion can lead to unique dilemmas where characters must navigate the intersection of magic and science, such as when technological advancements threaten to disrupt the balance of a magical ecosystem. By ensuring that consistent rules govern both elements, you can create a world that feels seamless, where both science and fantasy work together to enrich the narrative and offer intriguing challenges.

What scientific principles can be stretched or reimagined in your world?

Example: Gravity might be weaker in magical zones, or plants might grow through advanced bioengineering.

How do you ensure that fantastical elements feel integrated rather than arbitrary?

Example: Establish a set of consistent rules that govern both science and magic.

What narrative benefits arise from merging science and fantasy?

Example: Gravity might be weaker in magical zones, or plants might grow through advanced bioengineering.

Checkpoint

Let's pause. Gather your thoughts and answers from the previous section and use this checkpoint to put it all together. Summarize the extraordinary elements in your world. Use the following questions to help collect your ideas:

- Outline the rules and limitations that govern these extraordinary elements. What are the consequences when these rules are broken?

- Describe the unique flora, fauna, and mythical creatures you've created. How do they interact with the environment and society?

- Detail the architectural landmarks, monuments, and wonders.

- Summarize how your world handles time, space, and multiple dimensions.

Let's create some quick reference sheets that you can easily look back to while drafting your story. Fill in each category that fits your narrative. Remember: write only what you need—nothing more.

Landmarks

Special Artifacts/Objects

Social Daily Habits of the People

Unique Plants & Vegetation

The Laws of Physics

Unique Creatures

Medical Rules and Items

Objects as Reoccurring Symbols

Other:
(Be Creative)

Other:
(Be Creative)

Bringing it All Together

You've done the hard work: purpose, tone, map, myths, rules, creatures, and conflicts. Now it's time to pull those pieces together into something usable. This section is not another assignment—it's a quick toolkit to help you *see* how the elements interact and to make a one-page reference you'll actually use while drafting.

Start here: your world isn't the story—it's what shapes the story. Use this chapter to check that geography, history, economy, belief systems, rules, and special features fit together and point toward the same emotional truth. You'll make two practical pages: a concise world overview (two-page form) and an integration chart that shows how each major element affects plot and characters. Then run a short consistency checklist to catch anything that would confuse readers or trip you up later.

Do this in short bursts. Fill the forms with precise sentences and bullets. If you find something contradictory or irrelevant, revise the world note—don't invent more details. This is about trimming and aligning so your world pushes scenes and choices forward, rather than distracting from them.

Two-Page World Summary

World/Setting Name:

One-Line Premise (what makes this world unique):

Genre & Tone:

Primary Locations:

Cultural Hallmarks (beliefs, values, laws):

Historical (or Mythic) Foundations:

Unique Features (magic, science, creatures):

Two-Page World Summary

Protagonist:

Primary Conflict:

       Sub-conflict:

       Sub-conflict:

What does this world *force* your characters to do?

       Top 3 Resources:

         •

         •

         •

Major Social Structures/Power Holds:

  •   •

Two-Line Reminder: World-Building Statement:

Other Things to Remember (margin notes):

Integration Chart

This integration chart shows how each major element (land, myth, rules, etc.) *a ects plot and characters* briefly. Integration matters because seeing these links reveals whether your world pushes the story forward or decorates it.

How to use it: In the first column (on the left), list quick reference details for each element. In the middle column, describe how that element drives the story plot (or subplot. In the last column, explain how that element affects character decisions.

Integration Chart

Element (add quick, concrete details)	**Story Impact**	**Character Impact**
Geography/Climate:	*Example:* Flooding season forces migration routes and a supply shortage subplot	*Farmers must choose between selling land and raiding—this sharpens mistrust of the government.*
History/Myths:		
Social Structure(s):		

Integration Chart

Element
(add quick, concrete details)

Magic/Tech Rules:

Story Impact

Character Impact

Element
(add quick, concrete details)

Creatures/Ecosystems:

Story Impact

Character Impact

Element
(add quick, concrete details)

Economy/Resources:

Story Impact

Character Impact

Integration Chart

Element	Story Impact	Character Impact
(add quick, concrete details)		

Element	Story Impact	Character Impact
(add quick, concrete details)		

Element	Story Impact	Character Impact
(add quick, concrete details)		

Editing & Refining Descriptive Details

Taking the time to refine and edit your world-building details is crucial for creating a vivid and immersive setting. Descriptive language adds texture and atmosphere to the world, making it feel rich and multi-dimensional. However, without proper editing, descriptions can become cluttered or repetitive, detracting from the setting's impact. Refining these details ensures that every word serves a purpose, contributing to a cohesive and evocative world.

William Zinsser, author of *On Writing Well: The Classic Guide to Writing Nonfiction*, emphasized that the true craft of writing lies in the process of revision: "Rewriting is the essence of writing well—where the game is won or lost." Editing helps to maintain clarity. Overly complicated or vague descriptions can confuse readers, making it hard for them to engage with the setting fully. Eliminating redundancies also ensures that your writing remains focused, without unnecessary filler.

Revision Reminders

Use anchors.
Show claims with objects/ rituals, not exposition.

Repeat motifs.
Echo one object or color to tie scenes together.

Pick 2 signature sensations.
Choose one sound + one smell per major location.

Prioritize fixes.
If time is short, fix the two biggest consistency problems.

Trim redundancies.
Keep the strongest sensory image per paragraph.

Show, don't tell.
Replace one telling sentence per scene with a concrete image.

Consistency Checks & Checklist

Maintaining consistency within your world is essential to keeping it believable and immersive. If the rules of your world are illogical or constantly shifting, readers will struggle to connect with it. Every element of your world should make sense within the boundaries you've set. By continually checking for inconsistencies, you can maintain a world that feels coherent and well-thought-out.

Logic testing helps prevent contradictions and ensures that every detail works harmoniously within the established world. For instance, if your magic system allows for certain powers, those powers must remain consistent and adhere to the rules you've created, or risk confusing readers. Internal consistency also applies to geography, culture, and character behavior—if a city has a history of isolation, it should not behave in a way that contradicts this fact.

In addition, keeping track of changes through notes, maps, and timelines allows you to stay organized and avoid inconsistencies. By testing the logic of your world, you prevent small contradictions from snowballing into larger plot holes, ensuring your setting remains believable and immersive. It also strengthens your world-building, allowing readers to lose themselves in a setting that feels stable and trustworthy.

Consistency Checks & Checklist

This checklist is a short, tactical scan to catch contradictions before they become plot holes. **How to use:** scan each item; mark Yes/No. If No, write one brief corrective note. This prevents small contradictions from becoming plot holes.

☑ **Rules are consistent** (Tech, magic, etc.)

☑ **Causality holds** (A → B makes sense; no unexplained leaps).

☑ **Timeline & ages fi t** (events, character ages, generational gaps).

☑ **Resource logic works** (why trade routes exist; why certain regions prosper).

☑ **Cultural behavior aligns with history** (taboos, rituals traceable to events).

☑ **Sensory motifs are consistent** (colors, smells, textures recur where useful).

☑ **Showable anchors exist** for major claims (object/scene you can show instead of tell).

☑ **No contradictory place names/terms** (same thing called two different names).

☑ **Character actions follow social rules** (why they can/can't act as they do).

☑ **Reader needs vs. author knowledge balanced** (does the reader need to know X, or only you?).

Use this checklist as the fi rst stage of revision. Flag any unchecked items for future review.

Before You Go

You've made it to the end! You've stitched together mountains, habits, laws, and legends into something with weight and warmth. I strongly want to encourage you to take a break. Yes, I know, I've said this before but if you've made it here, you've done some very hard work. You deserve a break.

You've built a place that can move a story. Now, meet the scenes that are waiting inside it. Draft the ones that thrill or terrify you first—those are usually the truest. The first pass won't be perfect. It's not supposed to be! Trust that this new world you've created will deepen as you write into it. Go. Find the moments only you can write, and don't forget the importance of the ordinary things in life. I can't wait to read what you discover.

Works Referenced

Chiang, Ted. *Stories of Your Life and Others*. Tor Books, 2002.

García Márquez, Gabriel. *One Hundred Years of Solitude*. Translated by Gregory Rabassa, Harper & Row, 1970.

Hemingway, Ernest. *A Farewell to Arms*. Scribner, 2012.

Hosseini, Khaled. *The Kite Runner*. Riverhead Books, 2003.

Morrison, Toni. *Song of Solomon*. Alfred A. Knopf, 1977.

Lubbock, Percy. *The Craft of Fiction*. Charles Scribner's Sons, 1921.

Sayers, Dorothy L. *The Mind of the Maker*. Harper & Row, 1987.

Tolkien, J. R. R. *The Fellowship of the Ring: Being the First Part of The Lord of the Rings*. George Allen & Unwin, 1954.

Tolkien, J.R.R. *The Letters of J.R.R. Tolkien*. Edited by Humphrey Carpenter, Houghton Mifflin, 1981.

Tolkien, J. R. R. *The Lord of the Rings*. Houghton Mifflin, 1954–1955.

Updike, John. *Rabbit, Run*. Alfred A. Knopf, 1960.

Zinsser, William. *On Writing Well: The Classic Guide to Writing Nonfiction*. 30th Anniversary ed., Harper Perennial, 2006, p. 83.